SCARLET

AN *Every* ~~Girl~~ SHORT STORY
Woman

by
NICOLE LOUFAS

Also by Nicole Loufas

Thizz, A Love Story
Illusion of Ecstasy
The Lunam Series
Got Mine
Side Game
The Excursion: A vacation novella

This is a work of fiction. Names, characters, places, and incidents are either the product of the author's imagination or are used fictitiously. Any resemblance to actual events, organizations, or persons, whether living or dead is entirely coincidental.

Copyright © 2019 by Nicole Loufas
www.nicoleloufas.com

Editing by Laura Hull, Red Pen Princess

Except for the original material written by the author, all song titles and lyrics contained in this book are the property of the respective songwriters and copyright holders.

All rights reserved. No parts of this publication may be reproduced, stored in a retrieval system, or transmitted in any form or by any means, electronic, mechanical, photocopying, recording, or otherwise, without the prior written permission of the author except for the use of brief quotations in book reviews.

For the birds

One

I remove my gun, badge, and shoes, replacing them with street attire. The days of traveling to and from work in uniform have lost their swagger, along with the excitement of being on the force. The monotony of my day-to-day routine is killing me. I've cried wolf on two potential drug rings, and chased down a skateboarder so I could cite him for defacing public property. I go out every shift hoping for something—a robbery, a mugging, anything—to make me feel alive.

"Hey, sexy." Theresa walks into the locker room and sits in front of the locker beside mine. "Cocktails at The Holding Tank?"

"Not tonight." I dangle my make-up bag in her face. "I have plans."

"Am I ever going to meet Mr. Wonderful?" She begins undressing. "You realize I don't even know his name?"

Nobody knows about him, not even my sister. We've been dating two months and haven't gone public yet.

"Mr. Wonderful will do."

There is no better way to describe him. He has that *something* none of the others had. That wonderful thing everyone is searching for but can't quite find. Well, I did and I'm holding on to it for as long as I can.

"Come on, Scarlet. Just a first name."

Theresa is down to her bra and panties. Her body is superb: boobs a perfect C, tiny waist, flared hips. She's every man's wet dream. That's one reason I don't bring my guy around. Why would he stick it out with me when Theresa is available? As a former curvy girl, I still have insecurities when it comes to my body. Mr. Wonderful has slowly changed how I view myself. He likes my curves, the extra little something-something that jiggles when I run. With him, I leave the lights on.

"The first letter of his name then. There's no reason to be so secretive unless you have something to hide."

If I don't give my nosy ex-partner a crumb, she'll start to think something is wrong.

"M," I say and close my locker.

"First name or last name? Doesn't matter. I'll call him Mr. M." She pulls a purple Planet Fitness t-shirt over her head. "I'm throwing myself a dirty-thirty birthday party. I expect you to be there with Mr. M." She slams her locker.

"When is that again?"

"End of summer."

"I can't plan that far ahead." I sit down and buckle my wedges.

"Consider this a save-the-date."

"Aren't those for weddings?"

Theresa stands over me, hand on hip. "Can you put a muzzle on Debbie Downer and just say you'll be there?"

"*I'll* be there. I can't make promises for anyone else."

"Good enough." Theresa moves in for a hug. "Have an orgasm for me."

"Gross."

"I live vicariously through you these days. Nobody wants to pet my kitty." She purrs as she walks out the door.

"Seriously doubt that." I listen a moment to make sure she's really gone before I check my cell phone. I have a text from him.

Him: Your place

Our texts are limited to a few words.

Your place.

My place.

Wine.

Beer.

Pizza.

Chinese.

This is how we set up all of our dates.

Everything important is said in person. I learned my lesson when it comes to texting and oversharing on social media. Constant communication kills the magic. My heart soars when I hear my phone ding with a text that I know is from him. They don't come often, once a day, twice if I'm lucky. We don't spend hours texting back and forth about the tedium of our days. Once texts involve picking up dry-cleaning or whose turn it is to do the dishes—it's the beginning of the end. I want to live in the enchanted world we've created as long as possible.

The drive from the station to my home is less than ten minutes but feels like an eternity knowing he's waiting for me. I gave him a key after two weeks. It felt fast, but he didn't flinch. I took that a good sign.

His black convertible Audi is parked on the street in front of my house. I've told him a dozen times to park in the driveway. His car is worth twice as much as my Honda. Even though I'm going to give him shit about parking on the street, I like that he doesn't care. My ex-boyfriend was a gearhead. His car was his baby. I always came second to his big-block Chevy.

I park and take one last glance in the mirror.

Lips – red.

Hair – messy but he likes my naturally curly hair.

Teeth – food-free.

Breath – minty fresh.

I step out of the car and walk gingerly up the stone path to my bright red door. The smell of food makes my stomach growl.

He's cooking.

This is one of those moments, the ones when I want to whip out my cell phone and snap a picture of him standing in my little kitchen wearing an apron and holding a glass of wine. I'd caption it something like: He's a keeper.

A soft glow from the candles burning on the dining room table light the living room. I close the door and lock it. I don't call out. He knows I'm here. We say nothing, not until the moment is right. I start around the sofa towards the kitchen and feel a hand slide around my waist from behind. He presses on my stomach and pulls me against him.

He offers no words.

I have none.

We stay like this for a few minutes. Just breathing, enjoying the feel of our bodies pressed together. When he releases me, I try to turn around. He grabs me with both arms to prevent me from turning. I nod to let him know I understand.

No moving.

The candles flicker, something on the stove sizzles.

I don't move.

When he returns, I feel him behind me even though we don't touch. Something comes over my head and covers my eyes. *This is new.* I don't know if I'm comfortable with blindfolds. As a cop, I need to observe, analyze. I stop him before he can finish tying the strings behind my head.

"Wait," I whisper. Whispering feels appropriate. "Say something so I know it's you." I know it's him by the feel of his hands, his delicious smell. I want to hear his voice to confirm, it's the cop in me.

"I have a surprise."

His English is perfect, but in moments like this, when he isn't thinking, hints of his native language make their way to the surface. He makes me wish I'd paid better attention in Spanish class throughout high school. I get by, but there is nothing sexy about the way I speak his language.

He leads me to a chair. It isn't a long walk. It's safe to say I'm seated at the round table in my dining nook. The table is made for outdoors or a foyer, but it's all I could afford when I bought the house.

"Stay." He taps my shoulders.

I hear movement in the kitchen: glasses clinking, a bottle of wine is uncorked—it's music to my ears. When he returns, he sits at the chair opposite me. Our knees touch beneath the small table.

"It smells amazing." It's some sort of fish in a garlic butter sauce. I'd bet my badge it's shrimp. That isn't the only smell competing on the table. "Did you bake?"

He unties the blindfold. "Happy Anniversary."

My eyes take a few seconds to adjust.

He slides his hand over mine. "It's our two-month anniversary."

I've been trying to keep our relationship on a mature level. Two-month anniversaries are so middle school.

"This is really...sweet." I cringe as I speak. "I didn't realize we were celebrating milestones?"

His sun-kissed skin turns a slight shade of red. "It's corny, but I wanted an excuse to cook to for you." He lifts my hand to his lips. "I know how much you love brownies." He uses his finger to dig into the corner of the dish. "Open."

I obey his command, then close my mouth around his finger. I savor the chocolate and the taste of him.

"Mmmm." I suck his finger clean. "That was delicious."

He sucks my saliva from his finger. "I have big plans for those brownies later."

If this were a movie, I'd clear the table, sending my cheap IKEA plates crashing to the floor, covering the carpet in angel hair pasta and prawns. I'd ruin this dinner and skip straight to dessert.

"Shall we eat?" he suggests.

My fantasy is put on hold when my stomach reminds me we haven't eaten in nine hours. I place the napkin in my lap like I'm civilized. "It looks great."

I somehow make it through dinner without licking his fingers again. Just mine. Dinner is amazing.

"Is there anything you can't do?" I ask as we load the dishwasher. "You barely even made a mess." When I cook, there's evidence on the counters, walls, and floor for weeks.

"I can't ski." He places a pod in the dishwasher and closes the door.

What kind of man knows his way around a kitchen? A married one. Quit being paranoid, Scarlet. Single men have dishwashers too.

I play this game a lot—the one where I come up with reasons why this won't work out. It's a dangerous and exhausting game, one that will surely ruin my dreams.

"I tried to ski a few times as a kid and once when I was in college. It was a humbling experience."

This is the most he's ever disclosed of his past. The past is a sore spot for me; I bring it up as little as possible. We focus mainly on the present, rarely on the future.

"Where did you go to college?" I polish off the rest of my wine.

He picks up the bottle and refills my glass.

"I went to UC San Diego for a year, then I had to drop out to help my father with the family business." He appears to drink from his glass, but really, he's just wetting his lips. He does this often—pretends to drink. He'll indulge in a glass with dinner. I've never seen him finish a second. When I'm home for the night, a glass of wine is somewhere nearby. I don't even own a wine stopper. Let's be real, I don't need one.

"As a kid, I spent summers in Mexico working on the farm but I never thought I'd end up in the family business. After I left college, I went to work in the Imperial Beach distribution center. Been here ever since."

Arini Family Farms is one of the largest produce importers in California. Its website touts it as the oldest too. If you ask local law enforcement, the company was importing more than just corn and avocados. The Arinis are notorious and their history in Imperial Beach is riddled with folklore, from drug running up Smuggler's Gulch to importing illegal goods. I wasn't fazed when I learned who Marcus was; in fact, I kind of liked it. He was exciting and so different than any other man I've dated. Being a cop, I did my research. I couldn't find a single blemish on their record. Other than a small outbreak of salmonella in the early nineties, they're clean.

"Your family must be really close. I just have my sister, Cindy, and she's always off on some exotic trip with her rich boyfriend."

"Is that important to you? Money, exotic trips?"

"No, not at all. My last boyfriend was broke." I hate talking about my ex. Everyone's ex should be off limits.

"Well, you're in luck because my family does very well." He crosses the kitchen and places his glass on the counter beside me.

"I don't need a man to take care of me." I stand my ground, pretending his body heat isn't melting my insides.

He moves my hair and places a soft kiss on my forehead.

"Good, because I'm not looking for a pet."

"What are you looking for?"

He lifts me under my ass and sets me on the counter, so we're eye level.

"A partner."

He thinks I'm partner material. Holy fuck. Does that mean he's asking for more? The man did bake me brownies.

I see my Facebook relationship status change from *It's Complicated*, to *In a Relationship*.

"No more talking," he orders and carries me to the bedroom.

He frantically removes his clothes. I match his hurried demeanor and undress, tossing my clothes onto the floor. This isn't normal. We usually take our time undressing, savoring every second. His frantic need to be inside of me leads me to believe he's feeling vulnerable. Sex gives him control. I allow him to reign over my body. As he kisses and caresses, I marinate on every tidbit of information he's offered tonight. I flip the notes around in my head trying to form a logical conclusion. He shopped for groceries and made dinner. This wasn't a last-minute booty call. Tonight was special, important to him. I want to make it more special.

He's lost in the first moments of bliss as he moves in and out of me. I slow him down with a jerk of my hips. His eyes open.

"Are you okay?"

"Yes." I kiss his chin. "I want to try something new."

He grins and drops down to his elbows. I plant my right foot on the mattress and push off, rolling him onto his back. He grabs my hips and pulls me on top of him.

"No." I shake my head.

He's trying to read my next move like we're playing a game of chess.

I kiss him deeply and gently suck his tongue. His cock responds. Reluctantly, I leave his mouth and slide my naked body down his torso until my face is buried beneath the sheets. He smells like me. I may not own his heart, but his cock is mine. I kiss the tip before parting my lips and sucking him into my mouth. Most of him.

He moans and grips the sheets. I pause a few seconds, allowing him to gain control, then I repeat the ritual. *Kiss, open, suck.*

I feel him pulsing, he's ready to blow. I stroke him.

"Scarlet, no." He finds the top of my head under the covers. "I don't want to come."

"I want to do this." I plead for him to come in my mouth. *That's a first.*

He sits up, pulling his cock from my mouth. *Another first.*

"Is there something wrong?" I bite the inside of my cheek.

"Baby, no." He scoots closer and pulls me into his arms. "I don't want to finish like that. I don't want to do…that with you."

"I don't understand." I'm fully aware this conversation doesn't lead anywhere good. Explaining why he doesn't come during oral sex forces him to think of the women before me. "You don't like it?"

"Of course I like it." He kisses the top of my head. "Having a woman suck me off isn't something I live for. In fact, it's always been a thing women I don't care about have done." He's struggling to explain. "I vowed to stop giving myself away—my body, my mind—to useless women. Women who mean nothing to me."

My cop brain says whatever he's trying not to say is bad. I test my theory and try to pull away. His arms tighten. The red parrot tattooed on his shoulder flinches.

"Just say it," I snap. Patience is not one my virtues.

He takes my shoulders like he's going to scold me and searches my face like he's trying to send a telepathic message. "I wasn't looking for a relationship when I met you. My family is difficult and emotional when it comes to dating. Especially when the woman I'm seeing is…"

Is he really going to play the race card? My mother was African-American and my dad was Scottish. The only trait my mother passed to me was her unruly hair. I've never branded myself as black or white. I'm American. I'm human.

"So, what, your family is racist?"

"That isn't what I'm saying." He looks at me like I'm crazy. "My family is Mexican. They can't be racist."

"Anyone can be racist."

"Well, your race has nothing to do with their aversion to our relationship."

"Then what is it? I'm not a virgin? I'm not Catholic?"

He chuckles. "I wish it were that simple."

"How do you even know they won't like me? I've never met them."

He nods. "And I've never met your sister."

Checkmate.

"I didn't think we were at *meet the family* stage."

He shrugs. "I assumed you weren't ready—or willing—to introduce me. Maybe this was something casual to you." He looks at the bed when he speaks. "Like I was saying before, this wasn't supposed to be anything, just a little fun. But this isn't just fun, not anymore." He rubs my bare arm and angles towards me.

Someone push the panic button on my heart because it's beating at warp speed.

"I told you earlier I wasn't looking for a pet. Women who want to be taken care of. I'm tired of dating women with no drive. No ambition. That's the kind of woman my mother wants me to marry. An obedient baby factory."

His mother sounds like a bitch.

"I want an independent woman. Someone with a career and a home of her own." He looks around my tiny bedroom. "Someone who won't get sucked into the politics of my family."

My parents passed away within two years of each other. My dad first of a heart attack, then my mom of ovarian cancer that was caught too late. It's been just Cindy and me for nearly ten years. Cindy was only fifteen when Mom died. I became her guardian at eighteen. We struggled to make sure she finished high school. When she wanted to quit and work full time, I wouldn't allow her. I worked two fast-food jobs and nights at Target restocking shelves. We did it together. Then she met Mick, and he swept her off her feet. After kissing a lot of frogs, I gave up on the idea of finding my prince charming. Until now.

"Are you trying to ask me something?" I can't help the ginormous smile that's taken over my face. This is not how I pictured it in my mind.

First, I wouldn't be giving prince charming a blow job.

Second, a ring would be involved.

Since we're sitting in the middle of my bed totally naked, I don't think he's about to pull a ring from a hidden pocket.

"You have become a bright spot in my life. I'm ready to take this to the next level. Scarlet, I want you—"

"Yes!"

"I didn't finish."

"I don't care, the answer is yes." I jump into his arms, on the verge of happy tears. I don't need a ring…not now. We kiss, but it's brief.

"I need to call my mom and let her know."

I'm crestfallen when he gets out of bed and rummages for his phone on the floor. He's really not going to ask the question? Even worse, his first inclination is to call his mom?

"My family needs to prepare for guests. They like to put their best foot forward." He brings the phone to his ear and waits.

I get out of bed and dress in a t-shirt and shorts.

"Hola, Mama." He speaks too quickly for me to grasp every word of his conversation. I get enough.

I had it all wrong. He wasn't asking me to be Mrs. Marcus Arini. He was asking me to be his date at a family barbeque.

Relationship status: TBD

Two

The promenade is busy on Sunday mornings. I stand beneath Surfhenge, an art installation made of abstract surfboards at the entrance to Portwood Pier Plaza. Surfers weave past harried vendors setting up to sell everything from jewelry made from seashells to home-baked chocolate chip cookies.

Sunday morning jogs on the beach have been my thing since I moved to Imperial Beach from Los Angeles. At first, it was strictly exercise. I had gained fifteen pounds my first year on the job. Half-off at McDonald's and free donuts start to add up. I wish I could say the extra pounds were what ruined my first relationship but it was me. All me.

I met Elias in high school. When my parents died, he stood by me, kept me from falling apart. I followed him into this career, then I nearly got him killed.

After the academy, we both landed dream jobs in Los Angeles. I went straight to patrol, while he was assigned to a special task force. Elias grew up with some questionable dudes. His connections to street gangs afforded him the opportunity to help on a big case. It involved him going undercover in a Hawaiian biker gang. He'd lived on the Big Island until he was twelve, so Elias knew how to speak Hawaiian Pidgin, a slang dialect that gave him a free pass into the gang.

We'd go weeks without seeing each other or even talking on the phone. One day he showed up with flowers and a bottle of Hennessy. We spent the next twenty-six hours having drunk sex. In a moment of utter stupidity, I did something I will regret for the rest of my life. Elias was sleeping beside me, snoring softly the way he did. I positioned my phone above our heads and snapped a picture. Then I posted it on Instagram, tagging us both.

Elias was using his Instagram while undercover and my account was filled with pictures of me in uniform: snaps of my partner and me giving shout outs to our favorite café for giving us free coffee, a video of our unit doing the mannequin challenge—you name it, I'd documented it. I captioned the photo 'Sleeping bae' and posted it. By the time his alarm went off three hours later, his cover was blown, and I'd ruined both of our careers. He was reprimanded for being careless, and I was scolded for being an idiot.

Just to be safe, Elias was sent out of state in WITSEC, and I transferred to Imperial Beach. That was six years ago, but I still think of him almost every day, especially when I run. Running is my therapy. Sand beneath my feet, the ocean at my side, sun shining above—It doesn't get much better than that.

Today I'm not thinking of my past. I'm worried about my future, the near future. In a few hours, I'm meeting the Arini family. I can hear my captain now: *They're a crime family.* Allegations have been made, but no evidence has ever surfaced. In our line of work, without evidence, there is no crime. Accusations of racial profiling and straight prejudice are made daily. Accusing a successful and legitimate Mexican-American family business of criminal activity without evidence to back it up, would be a field day for the press.

I cut my run short so I have ample time to prep for the barbeque. Marcus insisted I don't cook anything or bring wine. It isn't that kind of barbeque. Whatever that means.

My outfit was another conversation. Marcus hinted that I should wear a dress. A dress. To a barbeque. My go-to for outdoor events is usually shorts or jeans. It's May, so the weather teeters on warm most days. Today is a mild seventy-two. Not dress weather. Still, I find myself perusing the fancy side of my closet. I land on a simple wrap dress from Old Navy. It's charcoal gray, ties on the side, and will pair well with the flats I plan to wear. I draw the line at heels. It's a barbeque. Even in flats, I look smoking hot in this dress, especially my boobs.

I insisted on driving myself to his family estate. Not so I can make a quick exit if needed, but because if I drive, I won't drink . There are plenty of officers who imbibe off duty and drive home, but I'm not one of them. The no tolerance for law enforcement rule is taken seriously in Imperial Beach. I can't afford another blemish on my record or to make a fool of myself in front of Marcus's family.

I text Marcus when I'm in the car, ready to go.

Me: On my way
Him: I can't wait to see you. Text me when you get here.

I start my crappy Honda and back up. A car honks and I slam on my brakes. I check my rearview mirror and find Theresa blocking my driveway.

She gets out of her Prius and taps on the roof of her car.

"Hello! I was sitting there for three minutes. What were you so engrossed in that you didn't even see me?" Her facial expression changes when I get out of the car. "Are you going to church or something?"

"No, I have...a thing. What are you doing here?"

"I was going to see if you wanted to catch a movie. Obviously, you plan to catch something else in that dress," she smarts. "I'll see you Monday."

Theresa pretends it's no biggie, but I can tell something is wrong.

"Wait, T." I walk around her car. "What's going on?"

"Nothing," she sighs. "It's just that we never hang out anymore. You're always with your mystery guy, and I'm... Just forget it. I'm in a mood. I think I'll go have hate sex with the guy from narcotics."

"That sounds horrible."

"He isn't that bad, actually. And he can cook." She gives one of her sassy grins. "You look amazing, Scarlet. I hope Mr. M is one of the good ones."

I feel guilty for keeping so many secrets from her. There really is no reason to continue. I'm going to meet his family. *Welcome to the next level.*

"Marcus," I tell her. "His name is Marcus Arini."

A slow smile spreads across her face. "Marcus is a sexy name."

"It is. He is."

"I'm going to google him." She closes her door and rolls the window down. "I'll have a full report for you on Monday."

"Of course you will."

Three

I arrive at the Arini Estate just after two o'clock. The circular driveway hosts an array of SUVs. My little Honda is so out of place. I squeeze behind Marcus's car and get out, strategically leaving my Chapstick in the center console. A Chapstick run to the car is always a great excuse to get away when you need a breather.

"You must be Scarlet." A man in dirty jeans and a plaid button up shirt greets me from the door. He's dressed casually, you know, like for a barbeque.

"I am." I put on my fake smile and pretend to be thrilled to meet him. "Is Marcus around?"

"He's out back playing with the birds. Come on, I'll bring you in." He steps aside, and I walk through the open double doors. "I'm Johnny Arini, Marcus's uncle."

I try my best to be cute, friendly, not cop-like at all. Even though I make mental notes of his height, build, and the color of his eyes.

```
John Arini, age 67
Height: 5' 10"
Weight: 215lbs
Eyes: Brown
Hair: Brown
```

```
Occupation: Co-owner and founder of Arini
Imports
```

"If you don't mind me asking—" He looks back with a curious smile. "I don't know your last name."

"Macaw."

"Like the bird?"

"Yep, like the bird."

"Interesting." He keeps walking.

People have been teasing me about my name since elementary school, none of them have used the word interesting.

Johnny leads me through the Mediterranean style home. The marble floor glistens in the afternoon sun, lighting a path through the house. The furniture, paintings, even the doors scream "Mexico." Natural wood and white walls with splashes of color. It smells like the best Mexican restaurant in town.

"That's the family crest." Johnny points to a symbol painted on the floor. I recognize it from the website. A bird weaved around the letter A.

"It's lovely."

We continue into a formal living room. "That fireplace was built by our great-great-grandfather. It was part of the original house. This house was built around it." He knocks on the wall. "Go ahead, you can touch it."

I walk across the marble floor to fondle a fireplace. Up close I can see the bricks are weathered and chipped; soot stains and cracks attest to its authenticity.

"It's amazing."

"It's Mexican," he boasts. We continue the tour of the house.

My phone buzzes in my hand. I know it's Marcus wondering where I am. I was supposed to text him when I arrived but Johnny hi-jacked me.

We finally stop at a set of French doors leading to the yard.

"And here we are," he announces. At least fifty people turn and look as I step onto the patio. None of them are Marcus.

"Where exactly is Marcus?" I whisper to Johnny.

"He's around. Go get some tamales before they're all gone."

Johnny walks in the direction of a beer keg.

I check my phone.

Him: What's your eta?

I reply with a photo of the yard.

None of the other men or women approach me as I wait for Marcus. They sit in silent judgement wondering why a girl like me is crashing the party. A dog runs around the side of the house and sniffs my feet. He's some kind of bully breed—tall, slobbery, scary.

"Hey, Nacho!" Johnny yells. "*Váyase.*"

The dog scampers towards the large brick barbeque in search of scraps.

"You like beer?" Johnny offers me one of the beers in his hand.

Fuck it. I need a drink.

"Yes, thanks."

"Tio, I see you've met Scarlet." Marcus places his arm around my waist. "I hope he wasn't harassing you." He kisses my cheek.

"He was showing me around the house." I take a sip of beer.

"*Linda tu chica. y arriesgado.*"

"*No quiero oírlo, tio.*"

Johnny's smile fades as he turns and walks away. A group of men and women wait for him to rejoin their circle to get the scoop on me.

"Is everything okay?"

My cop instincts tell me that was a heated exchange. I didn't catch what they were saying. Aside from my being beautiful. *Arriesgado,* I repeat to myself. I'll have to look that up later.

Marcus lifts the beer from my hand and drinks half the glass. "I'm not sure I can make it through the day sober," he confesses.

"That makes two of us."

Large trees give shade to the patio and the area where Johnny and his posse are judging me. The other side of the yard is filled with picnic-style tables and a playground.

"Johnny said you were playing with the birds. Is that code for something."

He shoots a look at his uncle. "No."

"Are you going to elaborate?"

"I'd rather show you."

We walk past the playground onto a dirt path lined with bushes as tall as Marcus.

"Must have been great playing hide-n-seek through here as a kid."

"We weren't allowed to play out here." Marcus takes my hand.

"Why not?"

He looks down and takes note of my shoes. "You dressed perfectly."

I stop and look at him in a pair of jeans and a black t-shirt. His parrot tattoo peeks from beneath his short sleeves.

"And so are you." I tug at his shirt. It's so tight, I can barely grasp a finger full of material.

"I'm not meeting your family for the first time."

"I'm going to pretend that doesn't sound super sexist." I keep walking.

He pulls me into his arms. "I didn't want them to have any excuse to hate you. Believe me, they just need one little thing, like tight jeans and dirty sneakers. I want them to love you—," his face turns serious, sexy, "—I want them to love you as much as I love you."

My heart sings along with the birds whistling nearby. One loud caw draws his attention.

"I want you to meet someone." A playful grin dances across his face, as he leads me down the path to what I can only describe as an aviary.

The melodic chirping grow more intense when the birds see us. I can barely hear Marcus speak.

"Those are blue-cheeked amazons." He points to the birds making all the noise.

"How many are in there?" The cage, if it can be called that, is massive, like something seen at the zoo.

"Six," he yells over the noise. "They get loud when they're excited."

We walk past enormous cages holding dozens of exotic parrots. Marcus is like a child showing off his toys. He names them all; I don't even pretend to remember them.

In the center of it all is small tree with a cage built around it. Marcus points to a branch midway to the top where a bright blue bird sits on one foot.

"This is a hyacinth macaw. The Spanish word for macaw is *guacamayo*. We call him Mayo."

"He's beautiful."

"He's nothing compared to her." He spins me around. A white octagon, at least fifteen feet high, sits beneath a beautiful eucalyptus tree. "That is a scarlet macaw." He presents the bird like a proud parent.

I've seen pictures of the macaw—I am her namesake—but I've never seen one in real life. Her head is bright red, with equally bright blue, and yellow wings.

"Scarlet Macaw, meet Linda."

Linda means 'cute' in Spanish but it's pronounced *lien-da*. The bird's name is a play on the English name.

He walks to her cage and places his finger through the bars. He makes a clicking sound, and the bird makes its way towards him. Marcus pulls something from a container hanging off the side of the cage.

"Out of the hundreds of birds my family has raised, she has always been my favorite."

"How old is she?"

"Twenty-nine, same as me." He offers her another seed. "My father got her the same year I was born."

"Are you breeders?"

Marcus stops fawning over the bird and turns back to me. "More like collectors. Technically, it's illegal to sell birds without a license." He wraps his arms around me. "On occasion, my father will sell a bird to one of his friends. That's a family secret. I'm trusting you will keep it."

"I promise not to tell." I kiss him, and Linda squawks in my ear. "I don't think she likes me."

"She is the least of your problems." Marcus takes my hands. "Come on, it's time to meet my mother."

We emerge from the path to a gang of curious faces. Marcus asks a woman in cut-off shorts and a dirty white tank top, where his mother is.

"*Donde esta, jefe?*"

The woman looks like she wants to slit my throat. "*Cocina.*"

"*Gracias.*" Marcus guides me around the girl like he's afraid she's going to attack me.

"Who is that?"

"Oh, she's a cousin."

"Really?" I look back at her dirty blonde hair and blue eyes.

The people scattered around the yard don't seem like family. A dozen or so kids play on the structure, a few older women sit at the tables shucking corn. Marcus didn't introduce me to any of them. Not a single one has shown any interest in meeting me. Except for Johnny.

"Which side of the family is she from? Your mom's or dad's?"

"What?" He opens the patio door. "I don't know. My dad's."

"Which is it—you don't know or your dad's?" I'm a cop, I expect direct answers.

He lets the door close. "Who cares." He kisses my cheek. "You're about to meet my mother. You're going to need to focus."

Four

I stop at the opening to the kitchen. It's as large as any restaurant kitchen I've ever seen. It smells like one too.

"Mama." Marcus walks in ahead of me. I grip his hand like we're walking on the edge of a cliff.

Several women, with the same eyes and smile, watch as we approach Mrs. Arini from behind. One pulls out a camera.

"*Que?*" She looks up wondering why the kitchen has gone quiet. She turns around and nearly drops the knife in her hand. "*Mijo!*"

"Mama, this is Scarlet." He presents me the way he did his bird.

"It's nice to meet you, Mrs. Arini." I hold out my hand.

She brings her hand to meet mine.

"*¡Ay!*" Marcus yells and removes the knife from her hand.

"Excuse me, I'm cooking." Her accent is thick and her tone unfriendly. "Nice to meet you." She offers a curt nod.

"I'm *Tia* Paulita." A friendly face smiles from across the kitchen. "You can call me Paula." The elderly woman shuffles around the butcher block to hug me then moves on to Marcus.

"Very pretty." She kisses Marcus on the cheek.

"*Gracias, tia.*"

Clearly, his aunt is the nice one.

"Are you married to Johnny?

"Que?" Paula looks at me like I'm crazy.

"I just assumed, since you're his aunt…"

Another lady babbles in Spanish then the kitchen erupts in laughter.

Marcus shakes his head. "Johnny is her brother."

"Oh, Jesus. I'm sorry." I try to laugh it off, but Mrs. Arini is scowling at me. She starts speaking really fast to Marcus.

I don't catch any words I understand, but I can tell the exchange isn't pleasant. She finally stops and turns back to chopping.

"She likes you," Marcus lies. "Come on, let's go get a drunk."

We settle at a table with a bottle of tequila.

"Worst case scenario, we sleep here." Marcus pours two shots. Then yells to a couple of kids to bring us an orange from one of the trees.

A boy climbs the tree like a pro, pulls a few down, and tosses them to his partner. They argue in Spanish about which one is best. I realize my comprehension of the language is elementary because I understand everything they're saying. The older looking one is trying to convince Marcus his orange is juicer, the other one says his mama is juicy. They begin to fight.

"*Basta!*" Marcus demands, and they stop. "*Mira.*" He hands them each a dollar then flicks his wrist. They run back to the playground.

"Whose kids are they?"

"Everyone's." Marcus dismisses the question as he pulls out a pocket knife and cuts an orange. "This tequila is pretty good. You won't need the orange but just in case." He winks.

I don't want to be a buzzkill, but I also don't want to sleep here tonight so I give Marcus a choice.

"I have a two-shot maximum. Either we take both now, or one now and one later. You decide."

It's still early. I'll work the alcohol out of my system by the time I leave.

"One now and one after." His playful expression makes me smile.

"After what?"

"After whatever."

I'm intrigued. The estate is vast, and there are a lot of secluded areas to sneak off to. My girly parts are hoping Marcus has a little sexy time planned for later. He places the shot in front of me along with an orange wedge.

"*Arriba.*" He lifts the glass above his head. "*Abajo.*" He lowers it just above the table. "*Al Centro.*" He moves it in front of me like to say cheers. "*Adentro!*" He takes the shot. "Now you."

"I don't want to do it alone," I pout. "Now you have to have another."

"No. I'm not wasting my second shot." He calls over some men from the other side of the yard and instructs them to bring a glass to have some tequila with me. He pours them each a shot and they toast in unison.

"*Arriba, abajo, al centro, adentro!*"

This time I drink mine. How could I not?

Marcus rewards them with the rest of the bottle.

"*Salud!*" they say as they return to their side of the yard.

"Hey, what about our second shot?" After that rousing toast, I'm ready to ditch my rule.

He moves to my side of the table. "Don't worry, there's more where that came from."

We watch the boys play soccer in the dirt, cheering when someone falls or makes a goal. When one of them skins a knee, he yells for his mother and runs around the side of the house. At this point I realize, other than the few women hanging all over Johnny and his crew, there are no women in the yard. Anxiety kicks in. I'm that one chick at a party who doesn't help—the one sitting in the same chair in the corner the entire night, watching the hostess work her ass off to make sure everyone has a drink, that the food isn't getting cold. I'm the lazy *puta*.

I check my phone for the time since I got here. It's almost four. I've seen men carry trays of cooked meat to the house three or four times. Other than tamales, chips and salsa are the only items on the table. The women in the kitchen are preparing a feast, which has to be done soon. I don't have much time to offer help.

"Should I go help your mom in the kitchen?"

"God, no." Marcus clutches my side. "My mother is very particular about who she lets in her *cocina*."

"I feel like I should be doing something."

"You are." He kisses my temple. "You're keeping me company."

"Marcus," I whine.

"You are a guest. Nothing is expected of you...yet." His mischievous smile makes my thighs warm. "It's still early. Nobody's even here yet."

"Seriously?"

"This fiesta is for my father. We always have a party when he returns from Mexico. Everyone should be here by sunset."

I stereotypically assumed his family gathered together every weekend. It never occurred to me to ask if this was a celebration or birthday.

"He's been gone three months, so today is a big deal. I can't wait for him to meet you. It's perfect."

The kids run to our table yelling in Spanish. They want Marcus to play with them. I can tell from their casual demeanor, it's something he often does with the boys.

"Go," I insist. "I'll be fine."

Marcus kisses me on the lips and the boys oh and awe.

"Vamos!" he yells and runs off to play.

Once Marcus is deep into the soccer game, I make my move. Under the false pretense that I'm looking for the bathroom, I go to the kitchen. I'm just outside the door when I hear a commotion. I look in and see Mrs. Arini in the arms of a man. She's telling him she missed him and that he looks fat.

The ladies leave, giving them a private reunion. Almost private. I stay just outside the door, listening, piecing together words and expressions. They speak too quickly or too low for me to make sense of anything they say. Suddenly the side door flies open and Johnny bursts in.

"Where's my son!" he yells.

Mr. Arini tries to calm him down. Whatever he's telling his brother isn't working. I catch a few words here and there. He was crossing the border at El Paso and was stopped.

Johnny argues his son wouldn't do that. He knows better. Mr. Arini says his personal truck broke down, so he was in a company truck—he drew attention. They lost a shipment. No—border patrol seized a shipment. I recognize the word from hearing it around the station - *apoderarse de.*

Why would border patrol seize a shipment of fruit?

Johnny starts yelling. He says Marcus's name several times, then another word I know—one I just learned today—guacamayo.

"What are you doing?" A heavily accented woman appears beside me. She looks into the kitchen, then back to me.

"I'm looking for the bathroom."

She points to the door on my right. She isn't polite, and her accent isn't really Spanish. Her blonde hair and blue eyes, sharp cheekbones, as sullen as they are, give her an Eastern European look.

"Thanks." I smile as friendly as I can. "I'm sorry, I didn't get your name."

"Anya."

"Of course," I smirk. "Do you work for the Arinis?"

Anya's cold blue eyes stare through me. If we were in a bar or on the street, I'd probably be worried. Then I remember—I'm a cop. She should be concerned. I'll bet all the money in my bank account she knows who I am and she doesn't like me.

Marcus and I rarely speak about my job. It's the last thing I want to do when we're together. I'm over telling war stories about vagrants and the occasional car theft. My job never seems to concern him. Why would it? He's not a criminal.

In the safety of the bathroom, I process the information I've just discovered. A shipment was seized, but what? I replay the conversation again, trying to recall something familiar. I open my phone and text Theresa. Her ex-boyfriend, the prick, works for Homeland Security, and he's stationed at the border in Imperial Beach.

Me: Favor – can you ask Pete if people illegally smuggle birds from Mexico?

Theresa: Uh, yeah. They smuggle them in water bottles it's horrible. Pete actually seized a shipment back in February. Why?

Me: Just curious.

I hear Marcus in the hallway, asking where I am.

Me: I have to go. Text you later. Kthxbye

Theresa: Wait! Why do you want to know? Does this have anything to do with Marcus?

Me: No, why? Did you find something?

Theresa is notorious for her stalking, I mean, investigative skills.

Theresa: Yes, but I think we should discuss in person. There's a lot.

Fuck my life. I knew he was too good to be true.

Me: Tell me now. I need to know.

It takes three minutes for her to reply.

Theresa: Arini Imports is currently under federal investigation. My fuck-buddy from narcotics let it slip when I told him you were going to meet Marcus Arini.

Oh, lord. I knew telling Theresa was a mistake. The woman can't keep her mouth shut. Gossip is in her DNA. I don't have time to dwell on her big mouth. I need to know what exactly they have on the Arinis and who is being investigated.

Theresa: They don't just import veggies. They dabble in prostitution, drugs, there's a long list of illegal goods. Be careful, Scar. If I were you, I'd come down with a bad case of diarrhea.

Ironically, Theresa would shit herself if she knew I was at his family's estate right now.

Me: Thanks, T. I'll text you when I get home.

I close my phone and sit on the toilet to contemplate my next move. An amazing, sexy, compassionate, man loves me, and I have to tell him we can never see each other again. Cops date ex-felons all the time. Dating a member of a smuggling operation draws a red flag. Technically, Marcus is innocent until proven guilty. If I hadn't seen the bird aviary in his parent's backyard, I might lean to the side of innocent. There is no possible way Marcus is oblivious to his family's illegal activity. He knows everything there is to know about those birds, even where they came from.

I exit the bathroom and find the hall empty, as well as the kitchen. Everyone is outside. My return to the backyard is inconspicuous. The main focus is on Mr. Arini. He takes his wife to the center the yard and yells something in Spanish.

It's a song. A ballad begins, and he offers her his hand. She takes it, and they start a dance. The gesture, their movements, the look on his face as he admires his wife—it's the most romantic thing I've ever seen.

"There you are." Marcus creeps up behind me. "Are you feeling okay?" He probably thinks I took a dump or puked. Either is better than the truth.

I clear my throat to prepare my act. "Actually, my throat—"

"Watch this." He points to his parents. "Papa is going to present her a flower. A single red rose. It's their thing. When he proposed to my mother, he was so poor he couldn't afford a ring or even a dozen roses. Just one. He gave it to her with a promise that if she said yes, one day he could give her a thousand roses. Even though he can afford to give her what he promised all at once, the gesture of bringing her a single rose renews his commitment to her."

"That's really beautiful, Marcus. But I'm not—"

Suddenly, someone yells Marcus's name.

"Please don't kill me," he says as he drags me to the center of the yard.

New faces, smiling ones, female ones, welcome me into their fold. They clap and whistle as Marcus presents me to his father.

"Papa, this is Scarlet Macaw." He smiles every time he says my name. "Fate brought us together." He rubs his hand over the tattoo on his arm.

The first time we met was at the Imperial Beach Farmers' Market. I stopped to buy avocados from his stand and asked him what kind of bird was tattooed on his arm. He told me it was his favorite bird—a scarlet macaw.

"Linda is my spirit animal, and you are my soulmate." He gets down on one knee. Takes my hand, and pulls a ring from his pocket. "This belonged to my *abuela*." He holds the ruby and diamond ring at the tip of my finger.

I feel so many emotions.

So many eyes on me.

"Scarlet Macaw," he laughs. "Will you do me the honor of becoming my wife?"

My hand is shaking. My heart is jackhammering. I've imagined this moment since I was a little girl playing princess.

Marcus is better than any prince Disney could create. He is the man of my dreams. I know with every fiber of my being that if I don't say yes, I will regret it for the rest of my life. Whatever becomes of the information Theresa gave me, I won't deny myself this moment.

"Yes," I cry. "Yes, I will be your wife."

He slides the ring on my finger then lifts me in the air.

"She said yes!" he yells in Spanish.

The crowd cheers as he spins me around.

I barely have time to catch my breath when someone hands me a shot glass. I get it now. He was saving the shot for this.

His father approaches and pats Marcus on the back. He tells him he's proud in Spanish. "Now, you will have your store."

I'm confused. "A store?"

"Yes, I've always wanted a pet store, specializing in birds."

So, I'm going to be the wife of a pet store owner. I can live with that. It's safe. As long as the birds are acquired legally.

"*Gracias, papa*. I won't let you down." Marcus shows an enormous amount of respect to his father.

"Welcome to the family, Scarlet. My boy, he loves you." Mr. Arini's smile feels warm and genuine. I can't imagine this man running an illegal bird smuggling operation.

I look through the crowd for Johnny and Anya. They're not part of the celebration. I recall the conversation from the kitchen; his son was arrested in El Paso. If I'm marrying into this family, I need to know why.

"I'm going to run to my car really quick. I forgot my Chapstick."

"I'll go with you."

"No, stay." I point to a group of men waiting to get his attention. "They want to congratulate you."

I spin the rock on my finger in circles as I make my way to the front of the house. Luckily, no one noticed when I emptied my shot glass in the dirt before the toast. I click my key fob and unlock the doors. The sun is below the mountains; my headlights shine on Marcus's Audi. He's blocked in by a Hummer, but I still have enough room to get out. I'm thinking one step ahead. I get in the car and lock the doors out of habit.

Me: T – I need to call you.

Two seconds later my phone rings.

"Please tell me you're home." Theresa sounds frantic.

"Not quite yet."

"I just got a call from Leon."

"Who's Leon?"

"My fuck-buddy!" She is exasperated. "They're moving on the Arinis tonight!"

"Wait, what do you mean?"

"The task force plans to make a huge bust at the Arini office in Imperial Beach and the residence. Someone flipped. They have a shitload of evidence against Marcus's father." She pauses so I can soak it all in. "He implicated Marcus too, Scar. I'm so sorry."

It has to be Johnny's son who flipped. Even if he's implicating Marcus out of spite, that's enough to have him arrested.

"At least things didn't get too serious, right?" Theresa is digging.

I stare at the ring on my finger. "Yeah, I'm lucky."

"Call me if you need anything. Ice cream, wine...I got you."

"Thank you, T."

We hang up, and I bang my head on the steering wheel. The horn honks and a boy's head pops up from the backseat of Marcus's car. Then a girl pops up. They look about fifteen.

"Sorry," I yell to them. They go back to making out.

There are kids here, innocent children. I know what happens when the feds raid—everyone goes to jail. They will destroy the house, impound all the cars. It doesn't matter when or how the birds arrived in this country, they will be considered evidence of a crime.

If I tell Marcus anything, even hint there is a raid, I will be aiding and abetting. Feds usually raid at night, to catch their suspects off-guard. I check the time on my phone, it's almost five. The sun will set within the hour. I have to get out of here.

Five

I return to the party, and Paula intercepts me.

"Come on, you have to meet the family." She drags me around the patio introducing me to newly arrived faces. I meet a dozen *tios* and *tias* whose names will end up on a list of known associates of the Arini crime family.

She introduces me to several children and a few teenagers, one of them I recognize from the Audi. He is sitting beside the girl from the backseat.

"This is my son, Gustavo." Paula kisses the top of his head. "And this is Rosa, his *ruca*."

"MA!" he yells, embarrassed.

"I'm kidding," she insists, then shakes her head behind Gustavo's back.

I find myself laughing with her when I should be warning her. Even when Gustavo and Rosa are released later, they will be listed as present during the raid, their names forever tainted in the system. Even worse, if Gustavo works for the business, he could go to jail too.

"*Mi amor*," Marcus calls to me. He stumbles when he moves from the dirt to the paved patio.

"Are you drunk?"

He holds his forefinger and thumb together. "Just a little."

The group of men behind him cheer in Spanish. "He's getting married, he needs a drink!" one of them yells.

He falls into my arms. "I told you I loved you today. And you didn't say it back."

I was wondering if he noticed.

"I don't say like to say it for the sake of saying it. It kills the magic."

In the past, I declared my love too quick and too often, forcing the men in my life to tell me they loved me after every call, every text. They became meaningless words.

"I don't get it."

"Because you're drunk. Come on, let's get you in a chair." I try to find an empty space, but people are everywhere, eating, drinking, celebrating our engagement.

Holy fuck, I'm engaged.

I find an empty room inside the house. It appears to be a game room, with a pool table and enormous flat screen tv. I unload Marcus on the leather sofa and fix my dress. I should get an Olympic medal for hauling a grown man while wearing wrap dress.

"I brought some coffee." Mrs. Arini walks in with a mug in her hand. "Come on, you're a man now. Quit acting like a stupid boy." She scolds him then turns to me. "If you need something, I'm in the kitchen."

"Actually—" I stop her hasty exit. "I don't know your first name."

"You can call me Mrs. Arini."

"Mama," Marcus whines.

"Valentina," she reluctantly discloses. "You can call me Valentina for now." She leaves the door cracked open.

It's a small victory, but I'll take it. Not that it matters. She'll hate me tomorrow; they all will. My phone tinkles, and I know it's Theresa. I can't answer it now, not in front of Marcus.

"Who's calling you?"

"Nobody. Just Theresa. Girl talk."

"Answer it, tell her the good news."

"Not a chance...I mean, not right now. She'll want to talk for an hour."

The recovery is believable.

"I want you to know I meant everything I said tonight. You're my soulmate, Scarlet." He rubs the bird on his arm. "Now my father has to make good on his promise."

He's chatty when he's drunk and I need information.

"What promise, baby?" I allow him to lay his head in my lap. I stroke his hair in hopes to stroke a little honestly out of him.

"The old man said when I found the woman I wanted to marry he would let me out of the business. I never really thought he would keep his word." He starts to laugh. "I gave him no choice now. He can't keep me close if I'm married to a cop." His laughter grows, and he starts to cough.

The little voice inside me says run.

He's using you to get out of his family business.

When I look at his sweet face, his red lips, and thick eyebrows—I don't care. He feels right, even though everything is about to go wrong.

"Here, drink this." I offer him the coffee. He needs to get sober.

"Thank you, *mi amor*." He sits up and gulps it down then hands the mug back to me. "I knew from the moment I saw you. Your name tag said Macaw. I knew then you were the one."

If we're being honest, I'd noticed him long before the day I stopped by his stand. Marcus is known as the hot avocado guy.

"Did you feel the same way about me? When did you know?"

"I'm not sure. Probably after the first night we spent together. I watched you sleep and thought I could stare at that face forever."

That's not a lie. I've wanted Marcus to be *the one* from the moment I handed him my phone number. I swore I wouldn't do anything to jinx us. I was so worried I would be the one to screw everything up, I didn't pay attention to the signs. How could I without stereotyping him, his family? Not every Mexican importer is a drug smuggler.

His eyes are glossy and heavy from the alcohol. Even though he's drunk, his expression is serious. "There are things about my family," he starts.

"You don't have to explain." I don't want him to confess a word. If he tells me anything about their illegal activity, I have to report it.

"I need you to know, Scarlet."

I place my fingers over his mouth. "Shhh. Not tonight. Let's just have tonight." I slide my hand around the back of his head and pull him to me.

We kiss a few times softly.

"I've never made out with a girl at my parents' house," he confesses.

"I'm your first."

"My first, my only." He kisses me again, this time with more control. He softly pulls me towards his lap.

"We can't," I whimper. "I want to, but not here."

"My car," he suggests.

I remember the teenagers in his backseat. "No, mine."

He takes me out a side door to avoid the party. The coffee and the crisp night air seem to have sobered him up. I click my alarm, and the doors unlock on my Honda. I pull the driver's seat forward and climb into the back. He follows me in, closing the door behind him.

"What if they come looking for us?" His family catching us in the backseat of my car should be the least of my problems.

"They won't." He unzips his jeans and pulls them down, exposing his hard-on.

I'm wet just looking at him. I could stare at *that* for the rest of my life. I don't have a lifetime. Just tonight. I bend down and kiss the top of his penis. He grips a handful of my hair. I open my mouth and allow him to slide inside. My teeth scrape his shaft as I work him in and out of my mouth. He doesn't seem to mind my teeth.

"Oh fuck, Scarlet. I love fucking love you." He mumbles declarations of love in between cussing and moaning. Unlike before, I don't want to finish him off. I want him inside of me.

I sit up when I feel him pulsing. I pull my panties off and straddle his lap. He slides in easily. I grip his head with both arms and allow him to control our movement. He forces me to go slow, lifting me then slowly lowering me onto to him. It's glorious torture. A tear slides down my face, then another. I'm going to miss this. Miss him. He's my everything. My knight in shining armor. My prince. And I'm going to let him be arrested.

"What's the matter?" he asks. "Am I hurting you?"

No, I'm going to hurt you.

He pauses and wipes my tears.

"Don't stop. I don't ever want this to end."

"It won't."

I cry harder, masking it behind moans of pleasure. I squeeze him tighter.

"We have forever." He forces me to look at him. "I love you, Scarlet. I'll love you forever."

The words spill out of me. "I love you. I do. So much. I'm so sorry."

"Baby, stop crying. Why are you sorry you love me?"

He doesn't understand. He doesn't know. I can't tell him. If I do, I'll lose my job, possibly my freedom. If I say nothing, I lose him. Either way, I don't win.

"Make love to me, Marcus."

His erection never falters, never lets me down. He angles himself so he can go deeper inside of me. I wrap my arms around the front seats and stare at the stars through my sunroof. The windows begin to fog, but the sunroof is clear. I count the stars as Marcus starts his final ascent.

"Look at me, baby," he commands. "I want to see your face when I come."

I place one hand behind his head the other I put on the roof of the car as leverage. We stare into each other's eyes, his eyes filled with love and lust. I'll never forget the look on his face when he comes. A man is never more vulnerable than in the few seconds after an orgasm. He holds me like I'm going to fly away.

"I love you so much, Scarlet." He kisses me softly.

If he's exonerated, we can be together. We'll move away from here, to another state. Hell, to another country. I'm thinking too far ahead. He hasn't even been arrested but I know it's coming. I know charges will be filed. There's enough evidence in the backyard to put him away for a long time. He even admitted to me that they sell birds from time to time. The only way for him to escape prison is if he flips. If he loves me as much as he says, maybe I can convince him to do it. If he goes down and I don't report what I saw here, what he's confessed—I go down too. For the second time in my life—I lose everything.

He pulls his shirt off and hands it to me so I can clean myself. I know the moment we exit this car, everything changes.

Marcus zips up his pants, then uses his fist to wipe the side window. "I think it's clear." He moves to open the door.

"Marcus, wait." I grab his bicep, the one with the scarlet macaw. His favorite bird. His spirit animal.

Maybe he's right. We are soulmates, fated to meet.

Destined to save each other.

Thanks

This story was originally written for the Cop Tales Anthology. All proceeds were donated to *Officer Down Memorial Page.* It was an honor to be included among authors like Abbi Glines, T.R. Cupak, Kat T. Masen, and Kimberly Knight. Find out more at www.odmp.org

Shout out to my hubs for giving me ten uninterrupted hours that one Saturday so I could finish this story.

My dog, Achilles, for always knowing the exact moment I get on a roll and choosing that moment to bark at the back door for fifteen minutes straight.

To everyone in **Nicole's Book Rehab**. Thank you so much for hanging around. I truly wouldn't be writing this line right now if it weren't you.

Laura Hull of Red Pen princess: I'm so happy this book brought us together.

About Nicole

Nicole Loufas lives in Northern California. She loves books, music festivals, and bloody marys. She prefers gin to wine and hates the smell of fried fish. She writes books in between letting her dog outside to bark at the wind.

Learn more at:
www.nicoleloufas.com
Instagram: @nicoleloufas
Facebook: Nicole Loufas, Author
Twitter: @nicoleloufas

Made in the USA
Middletown, DE
27 May 2022